17 YEARS OF A BOY

DEBJIT SARKAR

Dedication

I the author of the book Debjit Sarkar wants to dedicate this book to my lovely mother.

My mother is playing a great role from my birth till now.Its nothing much to dedicate this book to my mom for others but for me and my mother its a massive thing.

Contents

17 Years Of A Boy

WRITTEN BY

DEBJIT SARKAR
E-MAIL-thedsarkar2006@outlook.com
Phone no-7602166836

Foreword

MOTHER AND SON

Preface

GROWING CHILD

Acknowledgements

I got help from my family and teachers to write this book.They inspired me a lot and gave mental support.

Those persons have a great importance in complence the book.

These persons are-

1. My mother Mrs. Swarupa Majumdar Sarkar
2. My father Mr. Tanmay Sarkar
3. My uncle Mr. Prashenjit Sarkar
4. My uncle Dr.Malay Sarkar
5. My physics sir Utpalendu chakroborty

CHAPTER ONE

THE BIRTH

Birth is the first stage of a person's life.It's must be a rememberable moment for the parents.I heared from my mother about my birth.I was very lucky that I was born in **National Medical College** in Kolkata.

For my birth everyone was joyful in my family. At that time I got some VIP treatment from my parents . Everyone made a target for me to become a renouned doctor before gaining conciousness.Most of the day I the lazy child used to sleep ,cry to disturb my parents.I understand now that time life was joyful and tention free.Birth is one of the most important part of our life as the journey starts from **birth** and ends at **death.**

After some days my parents gave me a name, which is **Debjit Sarkar.**At the time of birth we have only the body and name is given by others but at death we have only the name(Popularity)and the body dissappears.

Birth is the learning phase for human.At that time we have no conciousness and have to learn many skills from the elders.

I was not much fast and accurate in learning skills like language learning and walking.With time to time I learned those skills efficiently.

The phase of **birth** starts from birth to 4 - 5 years old.The productivity at that time is the lowest of all time.This phase not the time of productivity,it's all about relaxing

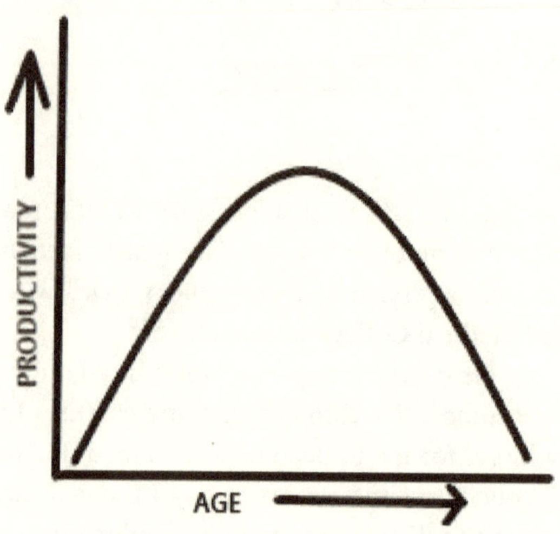

PRODUCTIVITY VS AGE GRAPH

CHAPTER TWO

GAINING CONCIOUSNESS

Conciousness is the second stage of life after birth.Without consciousness a person is not alive at all.At that time of being concious our productivity increases a slite. this phase goes from 6-8 years old. This phase contains begining of school life and education.At that time we balance study and play in a right way.

I Debjit Sarkar myself gaining theoritical consciousness at that time by going to school and from my parents.This was the time to do my works efficiently.I created a goal for my life to work on it instead.I wanted to be arenounrd doctor.Also a pressure is given from my family to do that which might be harmful for a child.That pressure makes a child anxious and decreases his productivity

In this time I learned and done everything efficiently to be a proper person.At the time of gaining consciousness we gain some habits which may be good or bad ones.At the time of creating good habits our consciousness is active but the time of creating bad ones our conciousness doesn't works.

One should never let his consciousnwss die in utter darkness because it is the most beautiful thing of our body as it helps to be different individuals.

As we are conscious animals we have many thoughts, some are good and some bad.So we have to **spot** the bad ones among all the thoughts and **stop** thinking about them and **swap** them with good thoughts.This technique is taken from book "Think Like A Monk" written by Jay Setty.The name of this method is '**SPOT-STOP-SWAP**'.

At the time of gaining consciousness many questions came in my mind which I used to ask to my parents.At the present day I think about those days which are such a good time.Conciousness is the missing link of our life we have to fill it with our intelligence.Consciousness is not about only being a responsible person its more about that thing.A casual person and a responsible person can have same consciousnes level.If you are conscious then you will never harm yourself passively or actively.

Gaining consciousness is the last stage in which we can leave carefree.After or during the stage we were admitted in school and with the start of school life pressure starts which increases gradually with time.

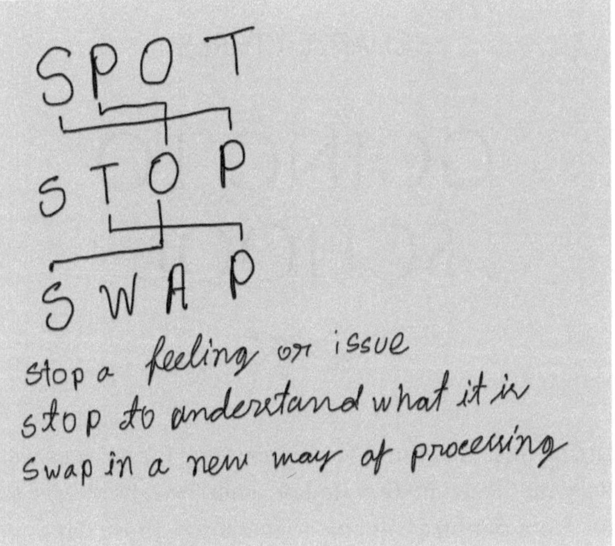

SPOT-STOP-SWAP METHOD

CHAPTER THREE

GOING TO SCHOOL

Starting of school life is very interesting for all of us.we can also remember our first day of school.we should get some time from our busy shedule to memorize those days.

I can memorise my first Day of school clearly,holding my fathers hand I went to school.I didn't cried on my first day of school though i was only 6 years old.I have a great score in primary school, every year I came second or first.Those days I used to teach by my mother who is a government primary school teacher.Everyone thinks thai i was a scoler student but reality was that my nmother made me scoler.

Iclearly understand now that practice makes a man perfect as I used to practice too much my studies that time.

PRACTICE VS PERFECTION GRAPH

One can notice that the potential is most when a boy reads in class 7 around.I completed my primary education at Shree Chaitanya Holy Child School
GOING TO HIGH SCHOOL-
At 10 years old I went to high school.I was admitted in Nabadwip Bakultala High School.The lowest class was 5 and height class was 12 in that school.So as usual I was nervous on my first day of going to high school.
I have so many friends in the starting of high school life but I don't know why the number of friends decreased with time. I noticed a downfall in studies after class seven but I can't resist it unfortunately. I can understand that the pressure was growing in my life time to time,class to class . Unfortunately COVID-19 came in 2020 when I was in class 8 to devastate my school life.I likely stopped studying at

that time . We all went to lockdown for approximately two years for COVID which disturbed our mental health as much as possible. We were not able to go outside at that time. I personally used to waste my time at that time which made a critical hit on my studies . It is one of the most difficult part of my high school life. For that covid 19 a new medium od education came, which is **online education.** It affected students massively. Students get distructed of social media and games as they take mobile from parents in the name of online class. After covid 19 our regular school started when i was in class 10

CHAPTER FOUR

PRESSURE OF BOARD EXAM

Now its class 10 and in my front there was board exam.At first I didn't gave attention to board exam but aftes 7 to 8 months i was serious about board exam.

At that time I had minimum 9 tution teachers ,for that my time of self study decreased very much and that affected my results of board exam.

The number gained in exam will increase gradually with the time you increase in self study. For easy understand its represented through a graph

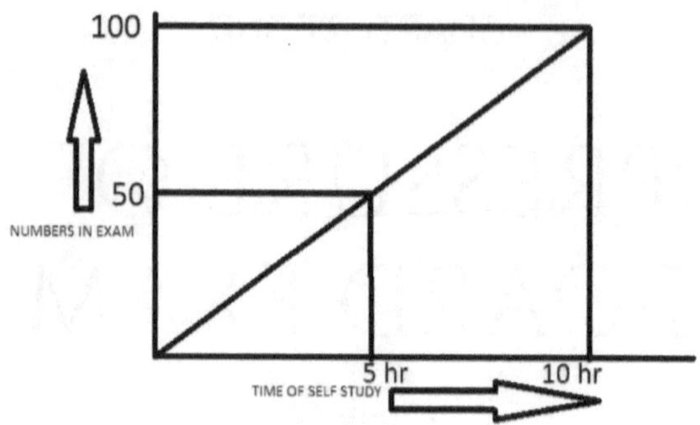

NUMBER VS SELF STUDY GRAPH

Board exams can feel like standing at the threshold of a significant milestone, with the weight of expectations bearing down heavily on students. These exams mark not just a test of academic knowledge, but often a pivotal moment that can shape future trajectories. The pressure associated with board exams is palpable, stemming from a variety of sources:

Parental and Societal Expectations: From a young age, students are often inundated with expectations from parents, relatives, teachers, and society at large. The pressure to excel in board exams can be immense, driven by the desire to meet these expectations and secure a promising future.

Competitive Environment: In many educational systems, board exams are highly competitive. Students often find themselves vying for top positions against peers who are equally driven and talented. The fear of falling behind or not performing up to par can add to the pressure.

Future Academic and Career Prospects: Board exam results can have far-reaching consequences on a student's academic and career trajectory. High scores can open doors to prestigious institutions and scholarships, while poor performance may limit options and opportunities. This knowledge can intensify the pressure to excel.

Personal Aspirations and Goals: Beyond external expectations, students often internalize their own aspirations and goals. Whether aiming for a specific university, career path, or personal achievement, the stakes of board exams can feel particularly high for those with ambitious dreams.

Fear of Failure: The fear of failure is a common source of pressure during board exams. The prospect of disappointing oneself or others, as well as the perceived repercussions of underperformance, can lead to heightened anxiety and stress.

Limited Time for Preparation: Board exams typically cover a vast syllabus, and students may feel overwhelmed by the sheer volume of material to master. Balancing preparation with other commitments such as school, extracurricular activities, and personal life can add to the pressure.

Peer Comparison: Students often compare themselves to their peers, whether in terms of study habits, academic achievements, or perceived intelligence. This culture of comparison can exacerbate feelings of inadequacy or intensify the pressure to measure up.

Emotional Well-being: The pressure of board exams can take a toll on students' emotional well-being. Anxiety, stress, and burnout are common experiences, impacting sleep, appetite, and overall mental health.

Despite the immense pressure surrounding board exams, it's important for students to remember that these exams are just one aspect of their journey. While they are undoubtedly significant, they do not define one's worth or potential. Seeking support from family, friends, teachers, and counselors can help students navigate this challenging period and maintain a healthy perspective on success and failure. Ultimately, what matters most is not just the outcome of the exams, but the growth, resilience, and learning that occur along the way

CHAPTER FIVE

LOSING GRAND PARENTS

Its natural to lose grandparents but for my case it was early.This type of incidents may disturb mental health.

Losing a grandparent is a profound and deeply personal experience, marking the end of a chapter filled with love, wisdom, and cherished memories. The grief that accompanies such a loss is unique, as it represents not only the passing of a beloved family member but also the loss of a connection to the past and the foundation of one's identity. Here's a reflection on the experience of losing grandparents:

A Deep Sense of Loss: The death of a grandparent can evoke a profound sense of loss that reverberates through every aspect of one's life. It's not just the absence of their physical presence but also the loss of their wisdom, guidance, and unconditional love that leaves a void in the heart.

Memories as Comfort: In the wake of their passing, memories of moments shared with grandparents become cherished treasures. From bedtime stories and Sunday dinners to quiet conversations and laughter-filled afternoons, these memories serve as sources of comfort and solace during moments of grief.

Reflection on Legacy: The loss of grandparents often prompts reflection on their legacy and the impact they had on our lives. Their values, traditions, and life lessons continue to shape our beliefs and behaviors, serving as a guiding light even in their absence.

Mixed Emotions: Grieving the loss of a grandparent can be a complex emotional journey, characterized by a mix of sadness, nostalgia, gratitude, and even relief, especially if they were suffering from illness. It's okay to experience a range of emotions and to give oneself permission to mourn in whatever way feels most authentic.

Support from Family: Family support plays a crucial role in navigating the grieving process. Coming together to share stories, offer comfort, and celebrate the life of the departed grandparent can provide a sense of belonging and solidarity during a time of loss.

Honoring Their Memory: Finding ways to honor the memory of a grandparent can be a healing and cathartic process. Whether through creating a memory book, planting a tree in their honor, or continuing cherished traditions, these acts of remembrance keep their spirit alive in our hearts.

Seeking Closure: Grieving the loss of a grandparent often involves seeking closure and finding meaning in the midst of pain. This may involve attending memorial services, visiting their final resting place, or engaging in rituals that provide a sense of closure and peace.

Continuing Their Legacy: One way to honor the legacy of a grandparent is to carry forward the values and traditions they held dear. Whether it's passing down family recipes, sharing stories with future generations, or embodying their spirit of kindness and generosity, we can keep their memory alive through our actions and choices.

Finding Healing: Healing from the loss of a grandparent is a gradual process that unfolds over time. It's important to be patient with oneself and to seek support from loved ones or **professional counselors if needed**. Finding healthy outlets for grief, such as journaling, art, or spending time in nature, can also aid in the healing process.

Celebrating Their Life: Ultimately, while the loss of a grandparent may leave a void in our lives, it also offers an opportunity to celebrate the richness of their life and the profound impact they had on those around them. By honoring their memory and carrying forward their legacy, we ensure that their love and wisdom continue to shine brightly in our lives and the lives of future generations.

My grandmother died first and then my grandfather between 3 months.My grandmother loved me very much.She always used to send gifts for me with my father. In my heart i have a lot of space for my grandmother

CHAPTER SIX

HAPPENING SOMETHING UNEXPECTED

Now I am in class 11 and have a pressure of neet exam . I joined online course and used to attend classes through my iPad. The use of iPad made me digital addict and I remember at that time I was not able to read books more than 30 minutes continuously.

What Is Digital Addiction-

Digital addiction, also known as technology addiction or internet addiction, refers to the excessive and compulsive use of digital devices and online platforms, leading to negative consequences in various aspects of life. It encompasses a range of behaviors, from constantly checking smartphones and social media accounts to spending long hours playing video games or browsing the internet.

One of the primary drivers of digital addiction is the accessibility and omnipresence of technology in modern society. With smartphones, tablets, and computers becoming integral parts of daily life, it's easier than ever to stay connected and entertained around the clock. The allure of instant communication, endless information, and immersive entertainment can be irresistible, often leading individuals to spend more time online than they intend to.

Digital addiction can manifest in different forms, including:

Social media addiction: Excessive use of platforms like Facebook, Instagram, Twitter, and TikTok for socializing, seeking validation, and comparing oneself to others. The constant need for likes, comments, and followers can create a cycle of validation-seeking behavior.

Gaming addiction: Spending excessive amounts of time playing video games, often to the detriment of other responsibilities and activities. Games with immersive worlds, competitive elements, and social interactions can be particularly addictive.

Internet addiction: Generalized overuse of the internet, including browsing aimlessly, consuming vast amounts of content, and compulsively checking emails or news feeds. The endless stream of information and entertainment can make it difficult for individuals to disengage.

Smartphone addiction: Excessive reliance on smartphones for communication, entertainment, and information. Constantly checking notifications, scrolling through apps, and feeling anxious when separated from the device are common symptoms.

Digital addiction can have significant negative effects on mental, emotional, and physical well-being. It can lead to:

Social isolation: Excessive screen time can replace face-to-face interactions, leading to feelings of loneliness and disconnection from real-life relationships.

Impaired cognitive function: Heavy internet use has been associated with decreased attention span, memory problems, and reduced ability to concentrate.

Sleep disturbances: The blue light emitted by screens can disrupt sleep patterns, leading to insomnia and fatigue.

Poor physical health: Sedentary behavior associated with excessive screen time can contribute to obesity, eye strain, and musculoskeletal issues.

Mental health disorders: Digital addiction has been linked to anxiety, depression, and other mental health issues, especially in vulnerable populations such as adolescents.

Addressing digital addiction requires a multifaceted approach involving awareness, self-regulation, and behavioral changes. Strategies to manage digital usage include setting boundaries, establishing screen-free times and zones, practicing mindfulness, engaging in offline activities, and seeking professional help if necessary. It's essential to strike a balance between the benefits of technology and the need for healthy, fulfilling real-life experiences.

CHAPTER SEVEN

TOUGH SITUATION

In the previous chapter you came to know about my digital addiction. At that time my parents were very much tenced about my future bucause I was far away than my study world.

Parents took me to our village house to live with my aunt and uncle and elder brother.They thought that it will help me to get out from digital addiction. But unfortunately they were totally wrong . The company of my uncle , aunt and elder brother made me aggresive, angry and low confidence level.

They made me ujnderstand that I cant do anything in my life they always demotivated and tourtured on me.

you can understand what a mental state was going at that time , so imagine my mental state , I will not tell you about it.........................

CHAPTER EIGHT

OVERCOMING EVERYTHING

Now I'm in class 12 a responcible boy about my studies and take care of my parents . Many great Personalities helped me to come out from that tough situation

Now I am going to tell the names of those in a list order-

1. Sycretist Dr. Gobindo Basak

2.My uncle Prosenjit Sarkar

3.Councellor Mohit Ranadip

4. Dr. Kamal Uddin

The process of overcoming everything is onging still now . I am very happy and proud that I started the process of overcoming everything.

The End

THANK YOU